The Puppy Diaries

Fairy-Tale Puppy Picnic

written by
Mitali Banerjee Ruths

art by
Aaliya Jaleel

BRANCHES
SCHOLASTIC INC.

To my pack: Drex, Leena, Sonya, Jubby, and Tux —MBR

For Naina, Fatima, and Hadia —AJ

If you purchased this book without a cover, you should be aware that this book is stolen property. It was reported as "unsold and destroyed" to the publisher, and neither the author nor the publisher has received any payment for this "stripped book."

Text copyright © 2024 by Mitali Banerjee Ruths
Art copyright © 2024 by Aaliya Jaleel

All rights reserved. Published by Scholastic Inc., *Publishers since 1920.* SCHOLASTIC, BRANCHES, and associated logos are trademarks and/or registered trademarks of Scholastic Inc.

The publisher does not have any control over and does not assume any responsibility for author or third-party websites or their content.

No part of this publication may be reproduced, stored in a retrieval system, or transmitted in any form or by any means, electronic, mechanical, photocopying, recording, or otherwise, without written permission of the publisher. For information regarding permission, write to Scholastic Inc., Attention: Permissions Department, 557 Broadway, New York, NY 10012.

This book is a work of fiction. Names, characters, places, and incidents are either the product of the author's imagination or are used fictitiously, and any resemblance to actual persons, living or dead, business establishments, events, or locales is entirely coincidental.

Library of Congress Cataloging-in-Publication Data

Names: Ruths, Mitali Banerjee, author. | Jaleel, Aaliya, illustrator. | Ruths, Mitali Banerjee. Party diaries ; 4.
Title: Fairy-Tale puppy picnic / written by Mitali Banerjee Ruths ; illustrated by Aaliya Jaleel.
Description: First edition. | New York : Branches/Scholastic, Inc., 2024. | Series: The party diaries ; 4 | Audience: Ages 5-7. | Audience: Grades K-2. | Summary: Priya plans a fairy-tale-themed party for her friend's rescue puppy, which will raise money to help African wild dogs—but with five invited dogs the party is likely to be chaotic.
Identifiers: LCCN 2023005814 (print) | LCCN 2023005815 (ebook) | ISBN 9781338896909 (paperback) | ISBN 9781338896916 (library binding) | ISBN 9781338896923 (ebk)
Subjects: LCSH: East Indian Americans—Juvenile fiction. | Parties—Juvenile fiction. | Dogs—Juvenile fiction. | Fund raising—Juvenile fiction. | Best friends—Juvenile fiction. | CYAC: East Indian Americans—Fiction. | Parties—Fiction. | Dogs—Fiction. | Fund raising—Fiction. | Best friends Fiction. | Friendship—Fiction. | LCGFT: Fiction.
Classification: LCC PZ7.1.R9 Fai 2024 (print) | LCC PZ7.1.R9 (ebook) |
   DDC 813.6 [Fic]—dc23/eng/20230613
LC record available at https://lccn.loc.gov/2023005814
LC ebook record available at https://lccn.loc.gov/2023005815

10 9 8 7 6 5 4 3 2 1   24 25 26 27 28

Printed in India   197
First edition, May 2024

Edited by Katie Carella
Book design by Maria Mercado

MIX
Paper from responsible sources
FSC
www.fsc.org
FSC® C043100

TABLE OF CONTENTS

VIP LIST
(Very Important People and Pups)

Ma
(My mom, also known as Reeta)

Priya
(Me!)

Baba
(My dad, also known as Ashok)

Dida
(My grandmother is my mom's mom.)

Samir
(My little brother, also known as Sammy)

My family!

Amir

Ethan

Maddie

Melissa

Dola

My friends!

Prince

Tux

Oggy

Ranger

Squid

Dr. Oluwatoyin
(Dola's mom)

Aunty Dayo
(Dola's Aunt)

Dola

Kofoworola
(Dola's cousin, also known as Kofo)

Dola's family!

PICNIC PLANS

Hello, world! Priya here. Guess what?

I started my own business. That makes me an entrepreneur *(on-tra-prun-oor)*. Guess what else? My dad uses that word a lot.

My daughter is an <u>entrepreneur</u>. She started a business called Priya's Parties.

I'm learning a lot about myself.

WHAT MAKES ME FEEL EMBARRASSED?

My dad telling everyone about me

Not feeling prepared

Making mistakes in front of people

Trying to dance

WHAT MAKES ME FEEL CONFIDENT?

Making a to-do list

Feeling prepared

Done!

Finishing something

Stretch!

Helping my friends

Here is my business card. A client made
these cards for me after I planned her party.

Priya's Parties

HELPING THE PLANET ONE AWESOME PARTY AT A TIME!

Priya Chakraborty
Founder and CEO

My business raises money for endangered
animals! Priya's Parties helped three animals
so far.

quokkas

pangolins

manatees

My friend Dola just asked me to plan a party.

I said yes right away. Then we talked after school today.

I've never planned a party with dog guests. But I'm up for a challenge!

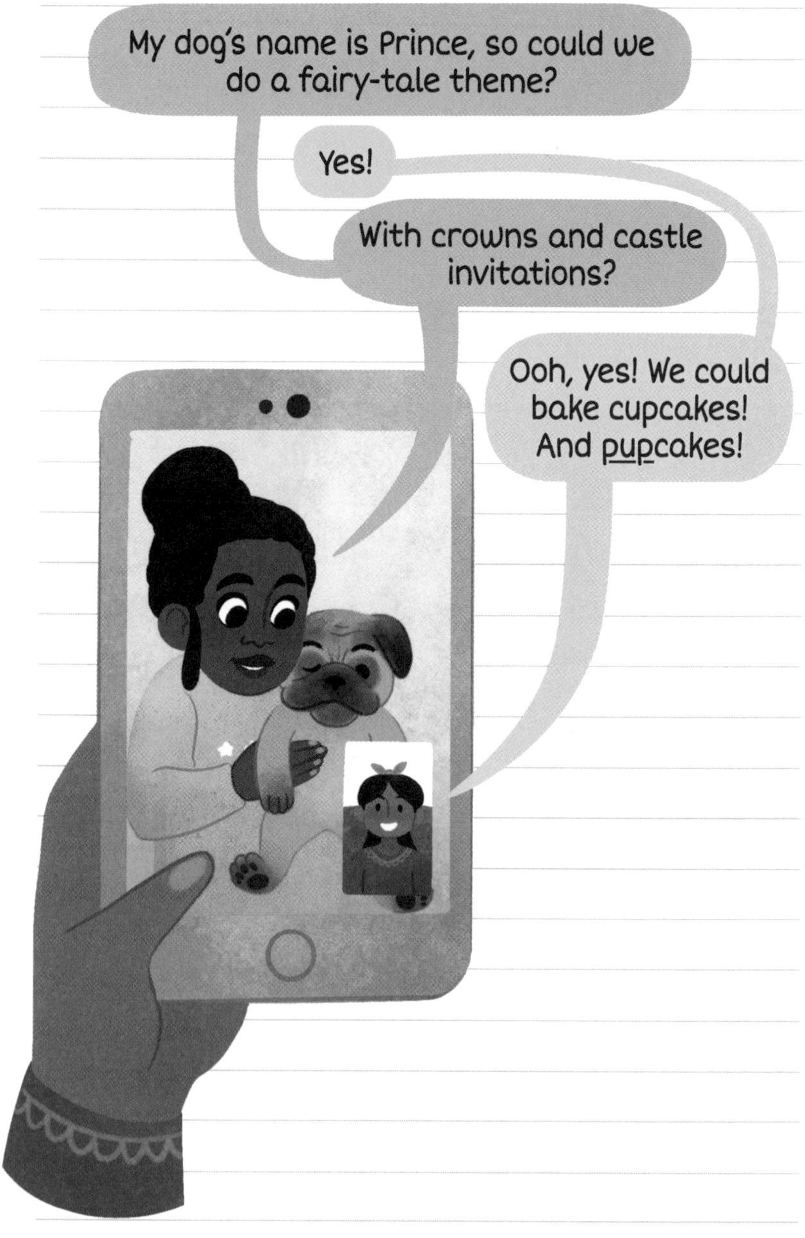
My dog's name is Prince, so could we do a fairy-tale theme?
Yes!
With crowns and castle invitations?
Ooh, yes! We could bake cupcakes! And pupcakes!

Dola is super-excited. That makes me excited, too!

I make a to-do list in my party diary.

Fairy-Tale Puppy Picnic To-Do List:

Make castle invitations.

Make crowns.

Make fairy-tale decorations.

Bake cupcakes for people.

Bake pupcakes for dogs.

HOW I'M FEELING

Excited! I have a party to plan!

Confident! I've planned awesome parties before.

Not confident! I don't have a dog. There might be important dog things I don't know!

So . . . I hope this party turns out happily ever after!

CASTLE CARDS

2

Friday

Dola, Melissa, and I head to my room. We're having an epic party-planning sleepover tonight!

Hey, Sammy!

Hello!

We get right to work.

PARTY PEOPLE:

Dola and Dola's mom
Kofo and Dola's aunt
Maddie
Amir
Ethan
Melissa
Priya

PARTY PUPS:

Prince
Oggy
Tux
Ranger
Squid

One name on Dola's guest list surprises me!

Ethan?

Yeah, he adopted his puppy from the same rescue place where I got Prince.

I don't know how to say this nicely, but Ethan annoys me. He laughs at his own jokes, and his jokes aren't very funny.

Priya packed a lunch of pickled peppers! Haha!

I'm NOT excited that Ethan is invited! But I don't say anything since it's Dola's party.

We need to make four invitations. (Dola, her mom, Melissa, and I don't need one.)

I cut this castle shape from a cereal box. So we can trace it.

Nice!

Melissa traces. Dola cuts. And I write on the invitations because I have neat handwriting.

I don't know anything about African wild dogs, so we look them up on my phone.

WHY AFRICAN WILD DOGS ARE SPECIAL

African wild dogs are one of the most endangered mammals on the planet! Their habitats in Africa are shrinking.

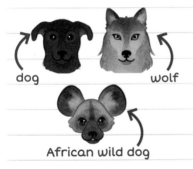

dog

wolf

African wild dog

African wild dogs are also called painted wolves. But they are not dogs or wolves!

The patterns on their fur are like fingerprints. No two dogs look the same!

They live in packs, or groups. They hunt together and look out for one another.

We finish the invitations.

You are hereby invited
to Dola and Prince's
FAIRY-TALE PUPPY PICNIC!
Sunny Grove Dog Park
Saturday at 11 a.m.

Hosted by Priya's Parties
to help African wild dogs!

These cards look great!

Yay! Take one for your cousin.

Priya and I can deliver the rest tomorrow.

It feels good to be done for today.

Sleepover Time!

Yay! I'm ready for pajamas!

One last thing! I write down a party-planning rule. I love coming up with rules so every party turns out AWESOME.

Take a Break Rule:

Make time to rest!

We get comfy. Melissa braids my hair.

You've got skills!

Thanks! I'm always braiding hair for dance.

Being with my friends gives me a cozy, happy feeling. I'm already excited for Sunday!

HOUSEKEEPING

3

Saturday

Today is Super Home Saturday. My family does chores together once a month. It doesn't sound awesome, but I have tricks to make it a little more fun.

CHORE GAME CHANGERS

Clean with music!

Oooh—mmm—mmm-yeah!

Race against time!

Will she set a new record for matching socks?

Work with a buddy!

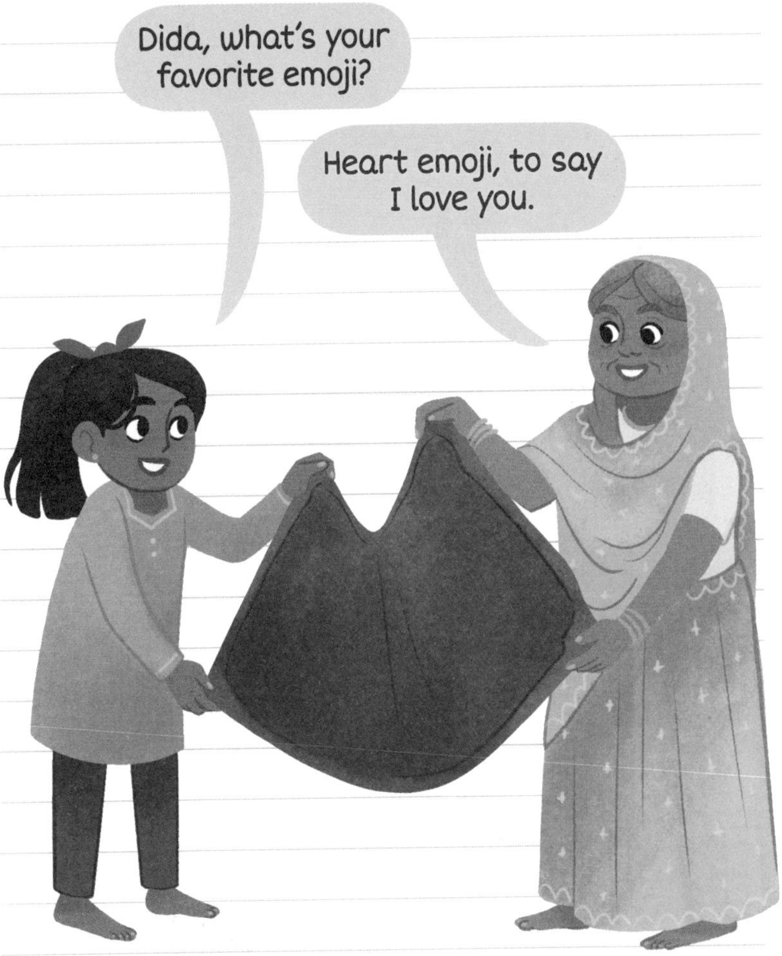
Dida, what's your favorite emoji?
Heart emoji, to say I love you.

After my chores, I text my friends to check in.

Dola, when should we come over tomorrow? I'll bring craft supplies. Do you have fabric we can use?

Come at ten! My mom's making lunch. She's got fabric.

Then I text Melissa.

My dad can drive us to Dola's tomorrow!

Great!

I can deliver invitations now.

Coming next door!

Melissa and I bike around the neighborhood. We leave invitations in Maddie's and Amir's mailboxes.

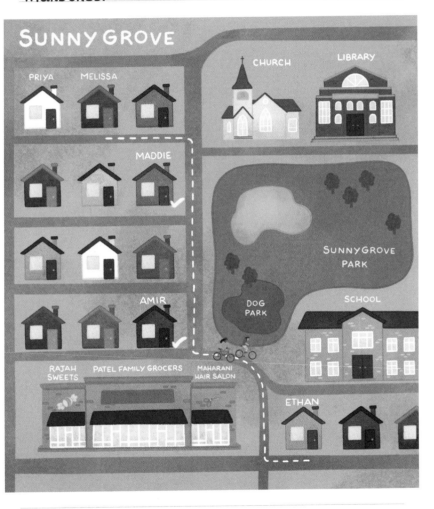

Our last stop is Ethan's house.

Ethan is out front playing with a small black dog. I yelp as it jumps on me.

Squid! Get off Pizza-riya! Haha!

Hey, Melissa!

Hey, Ethan. Here's your invitation for Dola's puppy picnic.

Dola told me about it. Nice castle. Hope this party is ROYALLY good. Haha!

As we bike home, I wonder if Ethan was being sarcastic. Sometimes people say one thing, but they mean something different.

Ethan said, "Nice castle." But did he mean, "That's a silly castle"?

Do you think Ethan hopes our party is bad, so he can laugh at me?

No. Stop worrying about what Ethan thinks.

This party will be royally GREAT! I hope.

FAIRY-TALE CRAFTS

Sunday Morning

Baba drives Melissa and me to Dola's house.

Um, you're carrying a lot.

Let us help.

I brought a lot of craft supplies.

★ Markers
★ Gems
★ Scissors
★ Cardboard
★ Paper

★ Beads
★ Buttons
★ Bottlecaps
★ String
★ Glue

recycled!

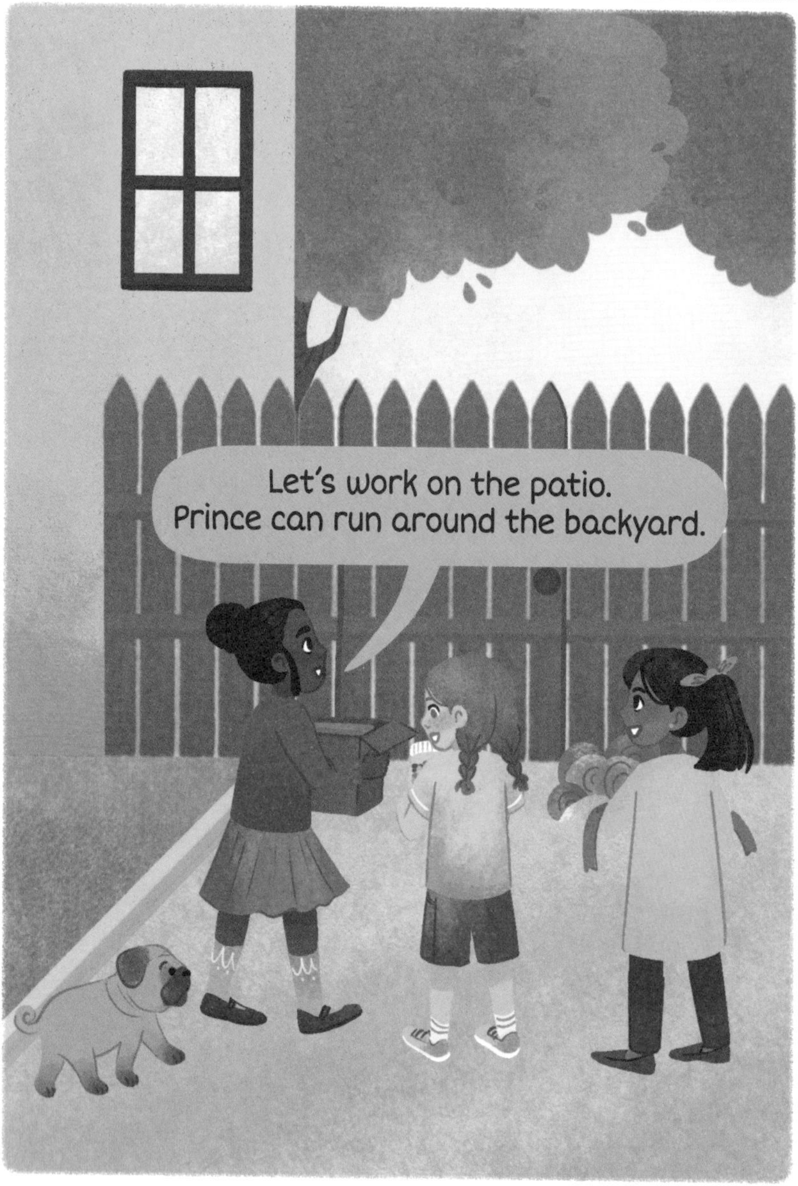
Let's work on the patio.
Prince can run around the backyard.

We start making crowns, but Prince doesn't leave us alone.

Prince rips a corner of cardboard.

We should make extra dog crowns.

Melissa gave me an idea for a party rule!

Plan for Extra Rule:

Have more than you need, just in case.

We need to get Prince away from the table.
I throw a stick. Prince brings it back. I throw it
again. He loves this game.

So, I multitask—I do two things at once. I
play fetch and I glue gems. Being around one
puppy takes so much energy. What will a party
with FIVE puppies be like?

I find extra-big pieces of cardboard.

Dola and Melissa finish the crowns. I finish two towers.

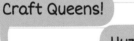

We're ready for lunch. Time to power up for more DIY!
(Do-It-Yourself)

CRAFTY EVER AFTER

5

Sunday Afternoon

The lunch food smells good! My stomach does a jumping jack. It's so happy.

jollof rice
cooked with tomato, pepper, and spices

coleslaw
shredded cabbage and carrot

fried plantain
crispy and sweet

I tried foods I never had before. My favorite were the puff-puffs!

After lunch, Dola's mom hands me fabric.

This cloth comes from Nigeria, the country where I grew up.

Dola's mom tells us about adire (uh-deer-ay). This type of cloth has a long history in West Africa. Artists draw with wax or tie the cloth with string to make designs. Then they use dried plant leaves to dye the cloth a blue indigo color. The wax creates adire eleko, and the string creates tie-dye patterns on the cloth.

Nigeria

wax pattern

string

plant leaves make a blue dye

adire eleko

tie-dye

We spread the fabric out on the table.

I show Dola and Melissa how to cut the fabric into strips.

We knot the strips onto a rope.

I hope our garland makes the park look like an enchanted forest!

I cross off most of my to-do list!

Fairy-Tale Puppy Picnic To-Do List:

- ♡ ~~Make castle invitations.~~
- ♡ ~~Make crowns.~~
- ♡ ~~Make fairy-tale decorations.~~
- ♡ Bake cupcakes for people.
- ♡ Bake pupcakes for dogs.

Craft Queens rule again!

Huzzah!

We're all set! On Friday, Dola will make party food with her mom. Melissa and I will bake at Melissa's house. I can't wait for Baking Friday and the party on Saturday!

SCHOOL DAZE

6

This week went by FAST. It's already Thursday!

Ethan overhears us talking.

Hey Priya-pickle! If it rains really hard, you could get extra party guests.

What?!

Well, it could rain CATS and dogs! Haha! Get it?

I'm telling myself not to panic about the party. But my mind races . . .

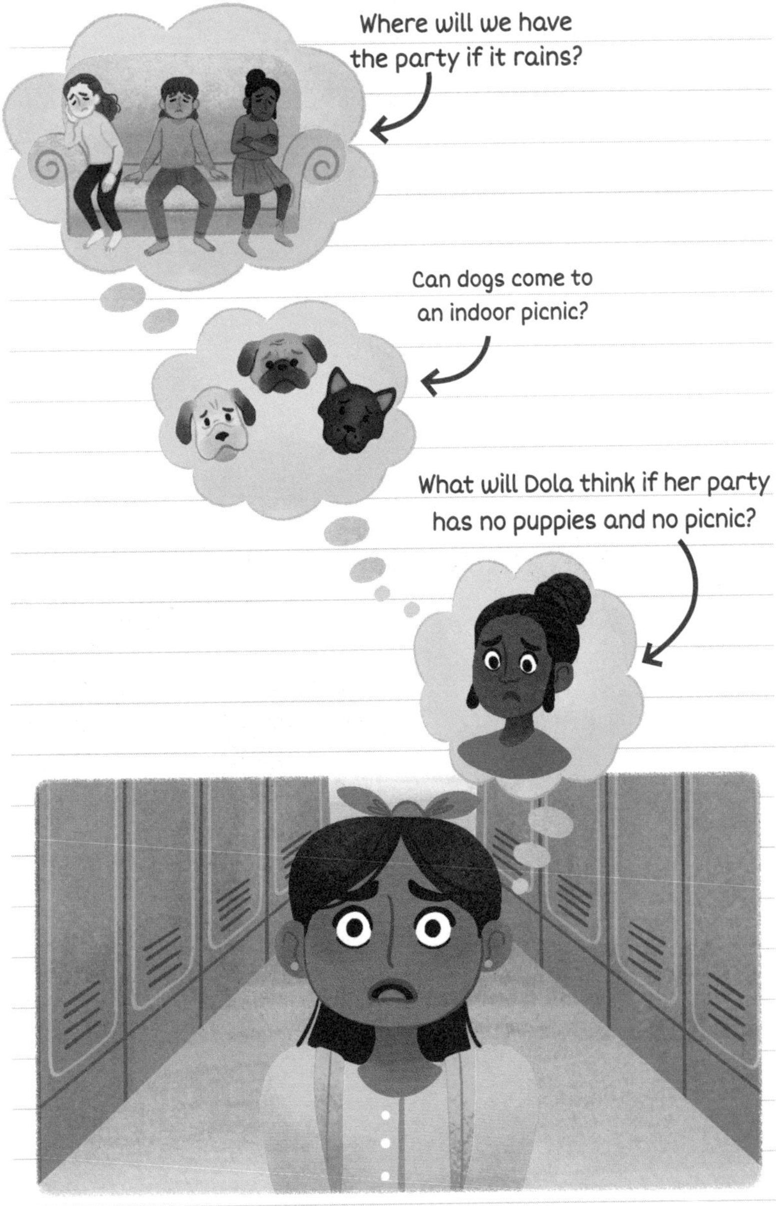
Where will we have the party if it rains?
Can dogs come to an indoor picnic?
What will Dola think if her party has no puppies and no picnic?

RAINY DAY BAKING

Friday

Today is Baking Friday. Melissa's dad picks us up from school. It's rainy.

I feel glum. That's the best word for it. I'm sad about the weather. It's like my heart is full of chewed-up gum that's being rained on.

Melissa tries to cheer me up.

She gets ruffly aprons . . .

takes out her
sprinkle collection . . .

and lets me
use the whisk.

Melissa's BFF (Best Friends
Forever)
magic works!
I feel less glum.

BFF MAGIC

We put the trays in the oven.

CUPCAKES	PUPCAKES
vanilla with sprinkles in the batter	whole wheat flour and peanut butter
Yummy for people!	Safe for dogs!

Next we draw and cut out fairy-tale objects. We'll stick them on toothpicks to decorate the cupcakes!

MAGIC ITEMS

wand

mirror

lamp

sword

book

key

You look worried.

What if it pours tomorrow? Everyone will get soaked. The dogs will get muddy . . .

I wait for Melissa to tell me not to worry. But she names MORE things that could go wrong!

The food will get wet! Our socks will get soggy!

We're playing a strange game about The Worst Thing That Could Happen. But it's weirdly making me feel better! ALL those things can't go wrong at once. Right?

Whatever happens, I'll be there with you—rain or shine!

Thanks, BFF!

MUD AND MAGIC

Saturday Morning

It rained all night . . . but it's not raining now!

Ma drops off Melissa and me at the park. We arrive an hour early with our cupcakes and pupcakes.

My phone buzzes.

Be there soon!

Two minutes later, Dola and her family arrive.

47

We get right to work. Melissa dries the picnic table. Dola and her mom set up the food. Kofo and I turn two trees into a pair of towers. Then we hang the fabric ribbon garland.

Welcome to Dola's Castle!

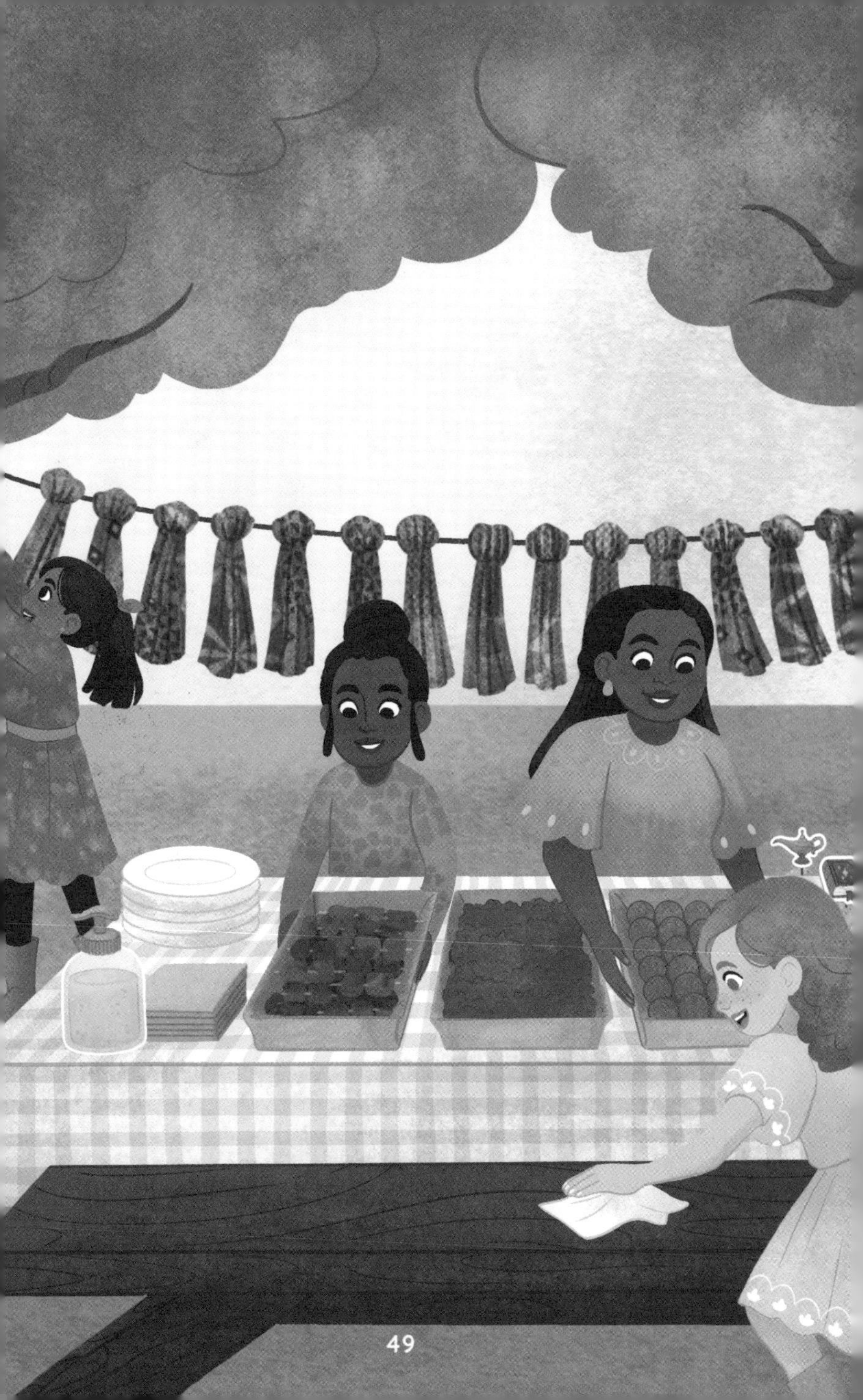

Ethan and Squid arrive ten minutes early. I didn't know dogs could wear rain boots. I let Squid jump on me because he's too adorable!

Wow, Priya! The park looks magical.

Ethan says my name the right way. He compliments the decorations. And he doesn't sound sarcastic! Am I in a fairy tale right now?

The rest of the guests arrive. Amir brought a Frisbee. People and puppies start playing.

What are the rules?

No rules!

Have fun and catch!

HOW I'M FEELING

Happy! Everyone looks like they're having fun.

Awkward! I'm not sure what I should be doing.

Brave? I'm going to play Frisbee, even though I'm not the best at catching!

Hey! I'm open!

Toss to Priya!

It feels good to go with the flow. I don't need to control or change anything about the party. I just need to be a part of it.

ONCE UPON A PICNIC

Saturday Afternoon

All the party people take a snack break. Then
Dola gets everyone's attention.

Everyone turns to look at me. I want to hide behind a castle tower, but I'm frozen.

Dola continues her big speech.

To celebrate this picnic, our family made a donation to help African wild dogs.

THANK YOU!

Everyone waits for me to say something. So I take a deep breath.

When people shine a light on me, I want to be someone who shines a light back.

Maybe it wasn't my best speech, but it came from the heart. Then out of nowhere . . .

The biggest dog I've ever seen charges into our fairy-tale picnic!

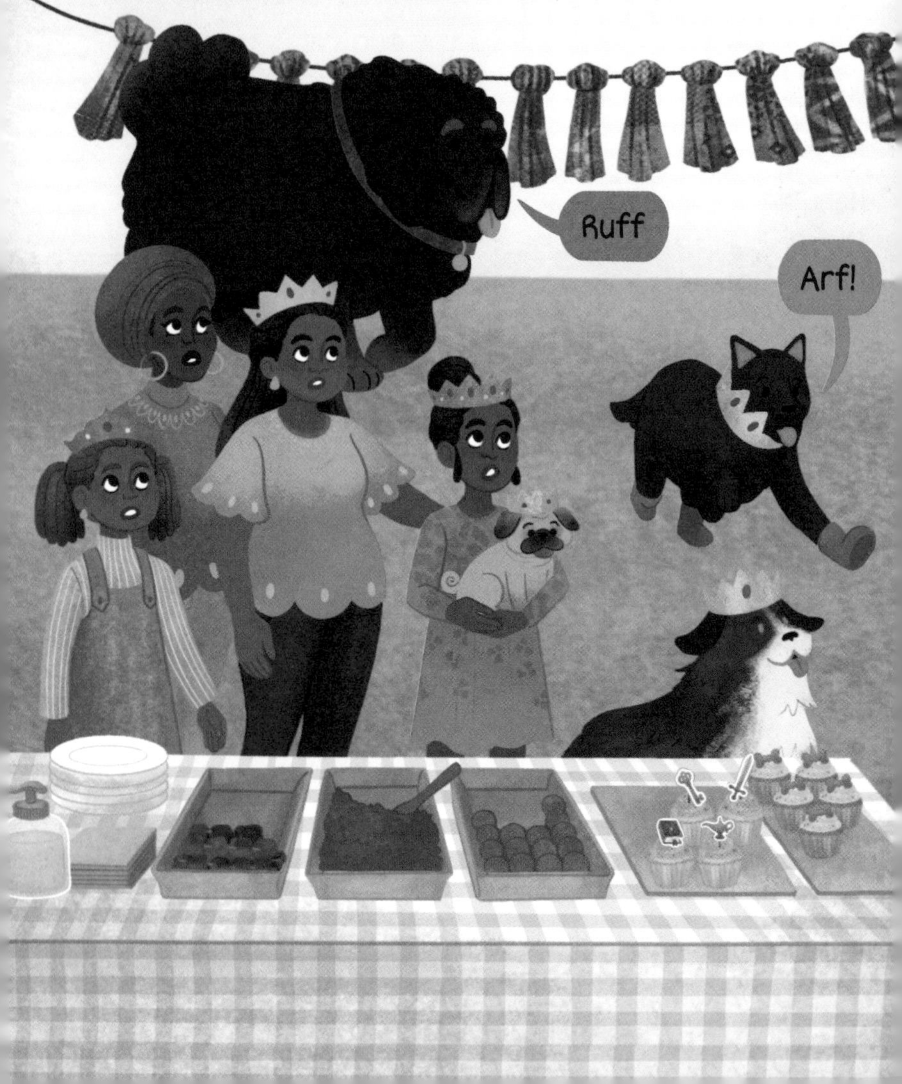
Ruff
Arf!

A teenager comes chasing after the dog.
Guess what?

I know him! It's Eddie! He came to a party I organized for his friend Tara. (She designed my business cards!)

Hey, Eddie!

Hey, Priya! Sit, Bongo! I'm putting your leash back on.

I go to get Bongo a pupcake.

And I find Amir eating one!

Amir! These are for dogs!

Oh! I thought it was a healthy muffin! Ranger can finish it.

Wait, what is Ranger eating?

Ranger was eating Oggy's crown. Amir says Ranger eats lots of things he shouldn't. They're working on that.

I give Bongo a pupcake before he leaves with Eddie.

Then I give Oggy a new crown.

Suddenly, Dola runs over.

This is a Worst Thing that I did not think about! My heart pounds.

We split up to look for Prince.

I pick up Prince's crown. I know it's his because I taped it to fit around his head!

My heart has not stopped pounding. Then Ethan spots Prince!

squirrel

I bet he chased that squirrel.

Everyone comes running.

Prince, I was so worried!

There you are!

We head back to the castle.

I got to see another side of Ethan today.
He can be helpful and . . . nice!

The party pups look tired. It's the perfect chance to take pictures!

Prince

Tux

Squid

Oggy

Ranger

The picnic ends PUPPILY ever after! Huzzah!

Melissa and I stay with Dola and her family to clean up.

I feel nervous before getting surprises. What could it be?!

NEXT UP

Saturday Late Afternoon

Dola and Kofo made me a thank-you gift!

This might be my cutest party yet!

Priya Chakraborty

Dola and Prince's fairy-tale puppy picnic was un-FUR-gettable!

Dola Abiola

Love the dog squad!

Kofoworola Robert

This party was PAW-some!

Dayo Oluwatoyin

I enjoyed meeting everyone!

Maddie Rose

Hey, Priya! Can you help me plan a fun sleepover party? You're invited, of course! 🐱

Yay! I can't wait to plan Maddie's sleepover with her!

DIY YOUR PARTY!
FABRIC RIBBON GARLAND

Use fabric scraps to make a fun decoration for your room or party.

WHAT YOU'LL NEED

- Fabric scraps (12 inches or longer)
- Ruler or tape measure
- String
- Sharp scissors

GET STARTED

1. Cut string to match the length of the garland you want. To make a garland that could hang over a standard door, measure string to about 36 inches.

2. Tie or tape the string between two chairs (or other sturdy objects). This will make step 4 easier!

3. Cut or rip the fabric scraps into strips to make fabric ribbons. Make the ribbons about 2 inches wide and 12 inches long. Or they can be a mix of sizes.

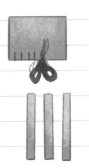

4. Fold one fabric ribbon in half. Hold the loop behind the string. Take the two ends of the fabric ribbon, fold them up, and pass them through the loop. This will make what's called a lark's head knot around the string.

5. Repeat steps 3 and 4 until you have knotted enough fabric ribbons to cover the string.

6. Trim the ends of the fabric ribbons.

PARTY TIME

Hang your garland to add a pop of color and joy to your room or party!

HOW MUCH DO YOU KNOW ABOUT
FAIRY-TALE PUPPY PICNIC

 1 Reread pages 24–25. What does "sarcastic" mean? Do you think Ethan was being sarcastic?

 2 At Dola's house, Priya tries foods she has never had before. Think about a time when you tried a new-to-you food. What did it taste like? Did you like it?

 3 On page 37, Priya says, "I can feel the stories inside this fabric." What do you think she means? Write about an object that holds stories for you.

 4 Priya feels worried about her party plans, so Melissa cheers her up! What thoughtful things does Melissa do for her? How do you cheer up your friends?

 5 What does Priya think about Ethan before the picnic? Does she feel the same way about him after the picnic? Reread page 66.

ABOUT THE CREATORS

Mitali Banerjee Ruths grew up in Texas and was a LOT like Priya when she was younger. She wanted to start a business, save the planet, and help endangered animals.

Mitali now lives in Canada. She still cares about animals, protecting the environment, and finding ways to be a better earthling. She admires how African wild dogs work together. Mitali loves working with others and helping her community!

This is Mitali's friend Tux!

Aaliya Jaleel loves illustrating books with bright, bold color palettes and exciting, lovable characters. When she is not drawing, she's planning fun parties that never quite go as planned—but that turn out memorable nonetheless.

Aaliya currently lives in Texas with her husband. She loves exploring and finding hidden treasures when traveling to new places.

The Party Diaries

Read more books!

The Party Diaries: Awesome Orange Birthday
written by Mitali Banerjee Ruths
art by Aaliya Jaleel
SCHOLASTIC
1

The Party Diaries: Starry Henna Night
written by Mitali Banerjee Ruths
art by Aaliya Jaleel
SCHOLASTIC
2

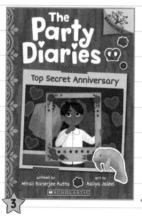

The Party Diaries: Top Secret Anniversary
written by Mitali Banerjee Ruths
art by Aaliya Jaleel
SCHOLASTIC
3

The Party Diaries: Fairy-Tale Puppy Picnic
written by Mitali Banerjee Ruths
art by Aaliya Jaleel
SCHOLASTIC
4